W9-DES-533

3 1160 00332 5532

STOP, THIEF!

BY **ROBERT KALAN**
PICTURES BY **YOSSI ABOLAFIA**

GREENWILLOW BOOKS, New York

Watercolor paints and a black pen were used for the
full-color art. The text type is Thaddeus.
Text copyright © 1993 by Robert Kalan
Illustrations copyright © 1993 by Yossi Abolafia
Printed in Singapore by Tien Wah Press
First Edition   10 9 8 7 6 5 4 3 2 1

Library of Congress Cataloging-in-Publication Data
Kalan, Robert,
   Stop, Thief! / By Robert Kalan ; pictures by Yossi Abolafia.
      p.   cm.
   Summary: A squirrel's nut changes hands several times
before returning to its rightful owner.
   ISBN 0-688-11876-3 (trade).   ISBN 0-688-11877-1 (lib. bdg.)
[1. Animals — Fiction.]
I. Abolafia, Yossi, ill.   II. Title.
PZ7.K12347SSt   1993   [E] — dc20
92-30081   CIP   AC

FOR MICHELE AND DANIEL
— R. K.

FOR CHEN
— Y. A.

That nut fell from my tree.

It's my nut !

I dug it up. It's my nut!
Stop, thief!

I can fly. You cannot.
It's my nut now.

This is my pond.

It's my nut now.

I can swim faster than you.